APPLES and ROBINS

by LUCIE FÉLIX

chronicle books · san francisco

All you need for apples

The apples hang high on my tree, just out of reach.

All you need for a ladder

are six rectangles:
five short

and you can climb into the leafy branches to pick an apple.

All you need to take a bite are two circles.

But someone else thinks so, too!
Ooo! A worm!

All you need for a bird are
three bright triangles like the robin's whistle
and a red oval like its round red breast.

It will fly away with the worm
and sit in my apple tree, singing.

All you need for a birdhouse

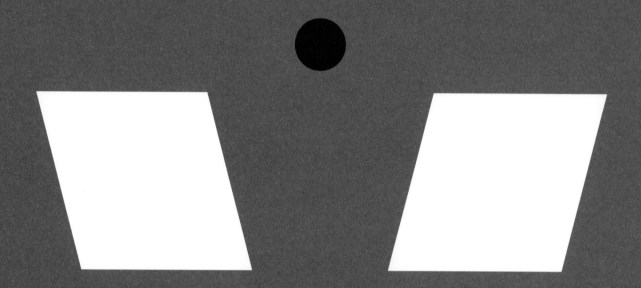

are walls and a roof

But all you need for a storm
is for the wind to blow . . .

CRACK!

Oh, what a mess!

But we'll rake the leaves
and gather the apples....

All you need for a basket . . .

is an empty place to put things.

And all you need for a birdhouse . . .

is a hammer and some nails.

I'll climb the ladder and hang the birdhouse
and take the apples in to eat.

All winter long there will be apples . . .

there will be robins.

And one morning,
when you are making your breakfast,

an egg will crack in the robin's nest.

There will be baby robins, and apple flowers.

It will be spring.